TRACEY CORDEROY

JOE BERGER

First published in the UK in 2015 by Nosy Crow Ltd
The Crow's Nest, 14 Baden Place
Crosby Row, London SE1 1YW, UK

5 7 9 10 8 6

A CIP catalogue record for this book will be available from the British Library.

Printed in Spain

Papers used by Nosy Crow are made from wood grown in
sustainable forests.

ISBN: 978 0 85763 529 7

www.nosycrow.com

CONTENTS

For Mark,
with love x
T.C.

For Will, Dylan, Jacob,
Tom and Eddie, with love x
J.B.

There was nothing Pandora loved more than spending time with her granny. Araminta Violet Crow was exciting, funny and kind. The only tiny problem was you never quite knew what she'd get up to next. You see, Pandora's granny was (whisper this next bit) … *a witch.*

The MESSY MONKEY BUSINESS!

Chapter One

"Hooray!"

Pandora skipped off the bus. She was on a school trip and her class had just arrived at SUNNY SMILES WILDLIFE PARK.

The park was brand new – opening today. The children couldn't wait to see the animals. And later on the Mayor would be coming too!

Pandora's teacher reminded the children

to be on their best behaviour.

"And no *monkey-business*," Mr Bibble told Granny.

Granny looked puzzled.

"I think he means magic," whispered Pandora.

Everyone set off to different parts of the park. Granny's group went to see the monkeys.

Problem was, when they got there, there wasn't a monkey in sight.

Nearby, a man was painting a fence.

"Where are the monkeys?" Pandora asked him.

"They're indoors until I've finished this," he said.

The children looked. The fence was so long. "But that'll take ages," they sighed.

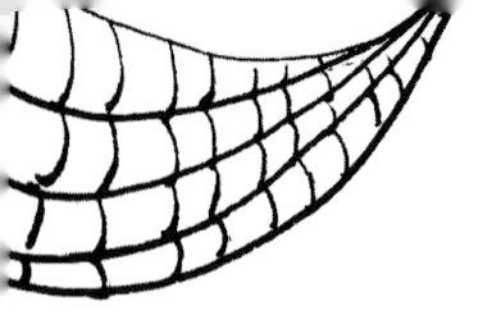

"Not if *we* help!" Granny smiled. "Mr Bibble said no *magic*, not no *painting*."

At once, she started dishing out paintbrushes.

"*Hang on…*" gasped the painter.

"Don't worry!" said Granny. "We'll be careful."

They began at once, really trying to be careful, but the paint kept running and dripping. And even with them all painting, it was still slow work.

"I think we need *more* help!" Granny said.

Grinning, she marched to the monkey-house and let out ALL the monkeys. "Monkeys are really fast painters," smiled Granny. "Watch this!"

The cheeky little monkeys swirled their brushes in the paint until they looked like drippy ice-lollies! Then they bounded off, chattering excitedly. "Ooo ooo ooo aaa aaa!"

Granny was right. Monkeys *were* fast painters. But they were very MESSY ones too!

They climbed as they painted. They swung as they painted. They dangled, leaped and tumbled as they painted. Soon paint was flying everywhere. Even Granny's *frog* got splattered.

"*Stop!*" cried the painter. But the children loved their helpers. And Granny thought their painting was great.

"The splatty look is just so *jungle*, don't you think!" she smiled.

When the fence was finished, the children were *covered* in paint, but no one cared a bit. Now it was time to play with the monkeys on their jungle-gym!

"Look at me!" cried Pandora, with an upside-down smile. Granny waved and Pandora waved back.

Never mind what Mr Bibble said, monkey-business was the BEST!

Chapter Two

Next they went to the Rainforest Zone, to see the reptiles, frogs and creepy crawlies. They were all behind thick glass windows.

"*Wicked!*" grinned Jake.

Inside an empty enclosure, a keeper was scattering a pile of leaves and bark around the cave floor.

"Why are you doing that?" Nellie asked her.

“To make it more *swampy*,” she smiled. “It needs to be just right for when the Komodo Dragons arrive later.”

“Can we help too?” Pandora asked.

“It’s quite muddy work…” the keeper smiled.

“Oh, they don’t mind mud,” Granny quickly chipped in.

"Well, in *that* case," grinned the keeper. "Come on in!"

Cheering, the children dived into the leaves like five excited little hedgehogs. Then grabbing great handfuls, they began to scatter them about the enclosure.

While they were busy, Granny watched the other creatures in the Rainforest Zone as they slithered, spat and clawed. The spiders were so cute with their hairy little tummies. And the *snakes*! "So huggy!" Granny smiled.

There were lots of frogs too.

"Poison dart frogs!" the keeper told Granny. "The more colourful they are, the more *poisonous*."

"Oooo!" gasped Granny. The frogs were really colourful!

As she and the keeper exchanged froggy tales, the children carried on with their job. But just before they finished, they ran out of leaves. So Pandora magicked up another pile. It was only a *small* spell, after all, and much easier than asking the keeper.

She also whisked up a gentle breeze to help spread the leaves about.

"Ooooh!" beamed Granny, turning around. "That's a good idea!"

Quickly, she whipped *her* wand out, too. "I'm a whizz at doing wind. Watch this!"

"Careful, Granny!" gulped Pandora. But it was too late. Granny had already waved the wand, and leaves were flying everywhere.

"Ooops!" she muttered. "Must have waved it too fast!" But just before Granny could sort things out, who should appear but … Mr Bibble.

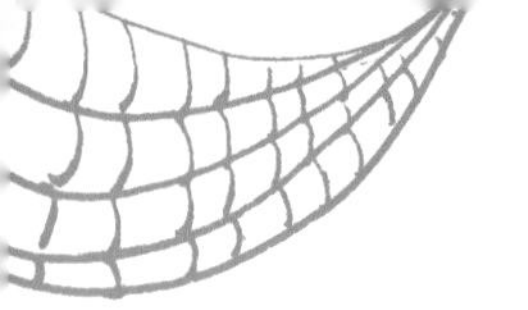

Pandora's teacher looked fit to explode as he battled his way through the storm.

"Stop it!" he yelled as leaves clung to him, making him look like a swamp-monster.

Granny swished her wand and the storm calmed at once. But calming the *teacher* proved trickier.

"Why are those children so muddy?" he snapped. "And why are they covered in paint! *How many ti—*"

But suddenly he stopped as the leaves behind Granny gave a rustle. Mr Bibble looked down and his eyes grew wide.

A *reptile* had escaped. It was a small and very colourful POISON DART FROG!

"Aaaagh!" screamed Mr Bibble. But Granny bent down and gently picked the frog up!

"This is no poison dart frog," she grinned. "It's just Croak – my little *pet* frog!"

She turned to Mr Bibble.

"Silly billy!"

Chapter Three

Now it was lunchtime. So Granny went to buy sandwiches. But the café only had plain cheese left.

"Oh," Granny groaned. Plain cheese was so DULL. But Mr Bibble had said "no more magic!"

"Pssst, Pandora!" she whispered. "Surely he won't mind if I add a small trumping tomato?"

"Better not," said Pandora. And Granny gave a sigh.

"If you say so…"

With that, the café door burst open and the sea-lion keeper dashed in.

"Oh, please – I need some help!" he cried. "The Mayor's on his way to watch the sea-lion show, but there are still a few things to get ready."

"Don't worry!" said Mr Bibble. "We'll give you a hand – come on, children!"

They raced outside and Granny went too.

"Hooray!" cheered the children. This was fun!

Some began topping-up the pool with water, while others found the sea-lions' toys. Pandora and her friends filled up buckets with fish.

The keeper said the sea lions *loved* their fishy snacks. But the children held their noses.

"Poo!"

Granny helped too by scrubbing down the benches the audience would sit on for the show.

But the water was freezing. And greasy. And grey. And the benches just wouldn't wipe clean!

Finally, she stopped and looked around. There were puddles everywhere, the toys had blown away, and the benches were still so icky.

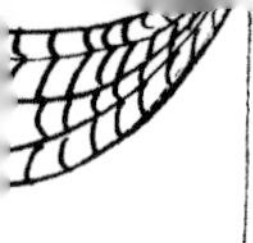

"Pandora!" whispered Granny. "If there is to be a show, I do think it's time to use my wand."

Pandora thought so too. "But you won't go … wild?"

"Me? Wild, dear?" Granny gave a wink. "Of course not!"

As soon as Mr Bibble popped inside to the loo, Granny quickly whipped out her wand. Then, with a flick, she whispered the spell…

"TIDY-UP-I-O!"

In the blink of an eye the place looked just perfect. The pool was now filled with twinkling water, the toys were all back in place, and Granny's icky benches glimmered like freshly-cleaned teeth!

The audience took their seats. Then the Mayor arrived too, and the happy little sea lions waddled out.

But wait! Granny frowned. The pool was missing something.

She had one last spell to do…

Granny waved her wand, and with a small bang! a huge, whizzy water-slide appeared.

Before you could stop them, the sea lions were all over it – slipping and sliding, zipping and zooming. Then splashing down into the water!

"Arc! Arc!" they hooted, and the audience tittered. What a fun way to start the show!

But not everyone was smiling. Mr Bibble

knew at once *exactly* where that slide had come from. Granny's wand had better stay in her *pocket* from now on!

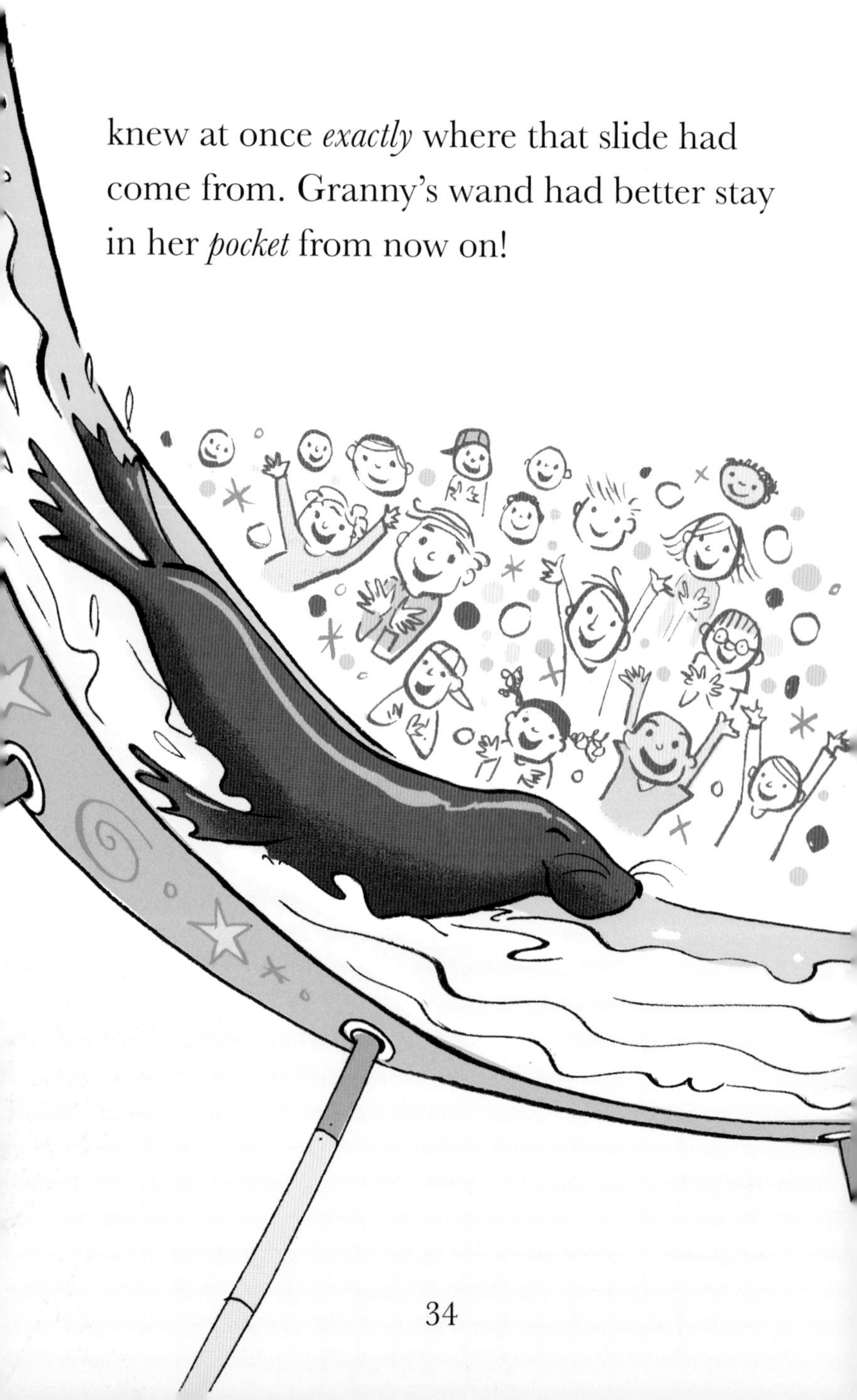

The sea-lion keeper wasn't bothered at all. As long as the sea lions and the audience were happy, that was just fine by him. So, picking up his microphone, he carried right on with the show! "Sea lions," he smiled, "are very interesting animals that can grow extremely large. They are found in oceans all over the world, and are hunted by killer whales and sharks. But neither of *those* are hiding in this pool … fingers crossed!"

Everyone laughed. And Pandora nudged Granny, who gave her a quick wink back. So far the show was going well.

But then it happened…

One of the sea lions got over-excited and shot down the slide *way* too fast. At the bottom, he flew through the air like a rocket.

"Arc! Arc!" he hooted as he turned three somersaults before landing in the crowd. But of ALL the people he *could* have splashed-down on…

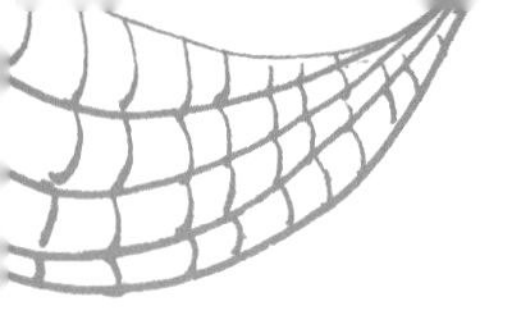

"Oh no," groaned Pandora. "Not the Mayor!"

The Mayor looked shocked to find a soggy sea lion in his lap. But...

"Hee! Hee! Hee!" he chuckled. He'd never seen anything quite so *funny*!

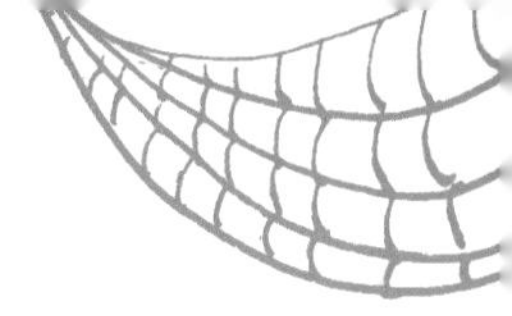

Suddenly the audience began to laugh, too.

Then everyone clapped, and clapped, and clapped – until even the *sea lions* were clapping!

The Mayor couldn't help but notice the children. They were painty, muddy, and very *soggy*. But he'd never seen such big smiles!

"What a wonderful place this is!" he said.

Pandora thought so, too. "Especially with *you* here," she whispered to Granny.

This was one school trip she'd *never* forget!

TODDLER TROUBLE!

Chapter One

Granny held up a pair of pyjamas she'd just covered in sparkly spiders.

"But Dad doesn't *like* spiders," Pandora said.

"Ahhh," smiled Granny. "But these are GROW-in-the-dark ones!"

With that, the doorbell rang so they zoomed downstairs

on Granny's broomstick. Granny peered through the door's frosted window.

"It looks like an *alien* has come to play!" she grinned.

They opened the door. But the alien was just *Max*, Pandora's next door neighbour. On his head was a small silver saucepan. And beside him his mum was holding his little brother, Sam.

"So sorry to bother you!" Mrs Higgins gasped, looking very bothered herself. "Max has been playing Pan Heads from Mars – *again*," she said with a sigh. "And he's got the saucepan stuck on his head again, too!"

"Well I—" began Granny.

But suddenly Sam was thrust into her arms. "Please!" squeaked Mrs Higgins. "Could you look after Sam while I nip Max down to the hospital?"

"No, listen—" said Granny, reaching for her wand. She could magic the pan off in a blink! But Mrs Higgins *wasn't* listening. She'd already scooped up Max and was hurrying off down the path.

"Thanks!" she called, dashing out through the gate. And they were gone.

Pandora and Granny exchanged glances. Sam was reaching for a big hairy spider dangling from Granny's hat.

"Um, Granny," said Pandora, her eyes fixed on Sam. "You know how to look after him, right?"

"Absolutely!" nodded Granny and the spider bounced closer. "And anyway – there's a *book* I bought your parents," she said. "Tells you all you need to know about tiddlers – I mean gobblers – I mean toddlers!"

They hurried back in to find the book and Granny popped Sam down.

"Granny – not in your *cauldron*," Pandora gasped.

"Err, what dear?" said Granny. "Ah-ha! Here's the book! *Dr Spook's Guide to Small Beings*!"

They flicked through the pages, quite forgetting Sam.

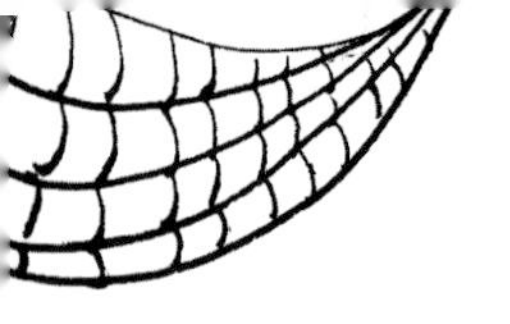

And when they turned to get him – he was gone!

"He's escaped!" shrieked Granny, dashing off to find him.

"Oh no…" groaned Pandora. "Wait for me!"

They tracked Sam down in the kitchen, where he was "playing" with Cobweb, Granny's cat. Except Cobweb liked playing with mice, not tail-pulling toddlers!

"Um, perhaps we should take Sam out?" said Pandora.

So Granny checked the book again.

"Yes – according to Dr Spook," she smiled, "toddlers love playing in haunted castles."

"Or maybe," said Pandora, closing the book, "we should just try the *playground* instead!"

Chapter Two

They were just setting off to the playground when Pandora suddenly stopped.

"Wait – Sam needs his *buggy* and his mum hasn't left it," she said.

Granny thought for a moment. Then she dashed outside, and came back with two frogs and a marrow.

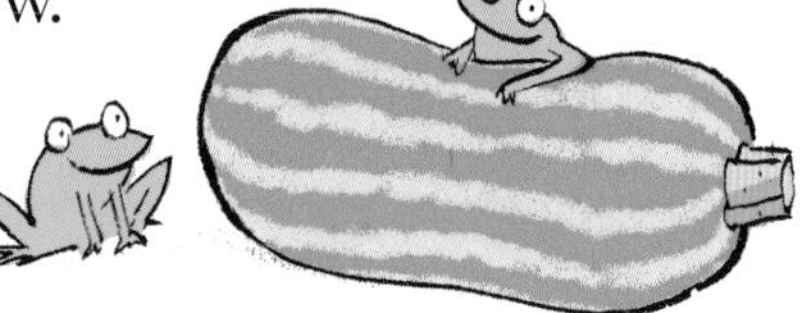

“But, Granny—” said Pandora.

“Just you watch!” Granny smiled.

She waved her wand and with a small **pop!** the marrow turned into a toddler-sized carriage, and the frogs into two miniature donkeys.

“There!” beamed Granny. “Much snazzier than a *buggy*, don’t you think!”

On the way to the playground Sam bumped along, squealing and jiggling excitedly. People stared, or had to leap out of his way.

The playground was busy. They parked Sam’s carriage then popped him on one of the baby-swings.

“Gooo-baa!” squealed Sam as Granny pushed him up to the clouds!

Next, he went on the roundabout. Granny went on, too. Nearby, some neat mummies were having a chat when a very windswept Granny whizzed by.

“Oh *my*,” sniffed one. “She’ll need a good hairdresser after that!”

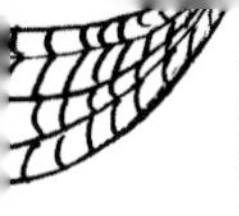

Pandora spied an ice-cream van so Granny bought three ice-creams. She was handing them out when…

"Wait!" she cried. "Where's Sam?!"

Sam had been right by their feet when they'd been choosing their flavour of ice-cream.

"I don't know!" said Pandora. They searched around but couldn't see him anywhere.

Then suddenly Pandora gave a squeak. "Up there!"

Sam had climbed to the top of the climbing-frame. And now he was stuck, and wobbling…

"Granny – he's falling!" Pandora gasped. But Granny was already waving her wand, and – *POP!* – the climbing-frame became a soft bouncy castle.

"Wow!" said Pandora.

Now, when Sam hit the floor, he just bounced back up again!

"It's just like a giant marshmallow!" Pandora giggled.

Granny came to the rescue in the sandpit too, when Sam *buried* himself. Granny's magic spades quickly dug him out, but covered the neat mummies in sand at the same time…

"So sorry!" cried Granny, about to clean it off. But Sam had found a sprinkler watering the grass, and – *whoosh!* – washed the sand off the mummies instead.

"Arggh!" they shrieked.

"Time to go…" gulped Pandora.

Granny thought so, too.

With a wave of her wand, everything was back to normal.

"Right then!" she smiled. "Lunchtime, I think. Follow me!"

Granny took them to a smart department store for lunch.

Pandora chose posh cod-and-chips, Granny chose posh squid-and-chips, and Sam had posh fish-fingers-and-chips, mushed three ways for toddlers.

It was going quite well

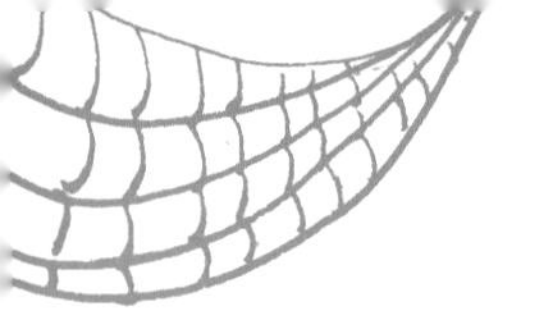

until Sam tried to feed himself, but fed a lady's handbag instead.

"Really!" shrieked the lady.

"So sorry!" gasped Granny. "It just fell off his spoon! Here – I'll clean it up!"

She jumped up to magic the mess away. But as she did, she jerked the table and a bottle of sauce tumbled into Sam's reach.

"Gooo-baa!" he squealed, shaking it so wildly that sauce went flying over *everyone*.

"I – ooops!" gulped Granny.

"Oh no," groaned Pandora as the manager came over and marched them to the door.

"I could clean—" began Granny.

But the restaurant door slammed behind them – BANG!

Back in the store's entrance hall, Granny looked glum.

"Maybe we could go to the toy department?" said Pandora.

She smiled at Granny, and Granny winked back.

"Why not!"

They turned to look for the lift. As they did, they saw to their horror that Sam had already found it. And the lift door was wide open and he was toddling in!

"Sam!" shrieked Granny.

"Stop!" yelled Pandora. "Wait for us!"

But it was too late. The lift door shut –

PING!

"We'll *lose* him," wailed Granny.

"We won't!" cried Pandora. "Look – there!"

She pointed to the display above the door. The number ONE had suddenly lit up.

"He's heading up!" cried Pandora. "Quick, Granny – to the stairs!"

They raced up to the first floor.

But the lift door didn't open! Instead the TWO above the door lit up.

"Back to the stairs!" cried Pandora.

But the lift stayed shut on the second floor as well. And on the third, fourth, fifth and sixth!

Then FINALLY, on the seventh floor – PING! – the door opened and a crowd of customers dashed out. They were coughing and spluttering and holding their noses.

"What—?"

But Granny stopped as the *pongiest* smell came wafting out of the lift after them.

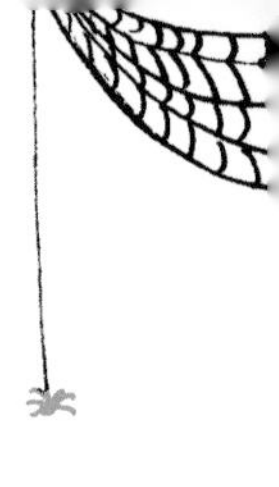

"Ewww!" squeaked Pandora, peeping in at Sam. "I think he's done a poo in his nappy!"

Granny picked Sam up and held him out at arm's length.

"Now what?" she said.

Pandora looked around. "Quick! There's a changing room – there!"

"*Good idea!*" spluttered Granny, heading on in. "But what shall we change him *into*? A teapot? A vase? And won't his *mum* mind?"

"No, Granny!" laughed Pandora. "We don't change *him* – just his nappy!"

After changing Sam's nappy, it was time to take him home.

Granny was exhausted. And although she liked Sam, she couldn't *wait* to hand him back and put her feet up. She might even treat herself to a nice cup of tadpole-tea!

They were heading out through the kitchen department when suddenly Pandora stopped.

"Look, Granny!" she said. Mrs Higgins and Max were wandering round looking for something.

"Yoo-hoo!" called Granny, and they hurried across to see them.

"Hello!" said Granny. "Fancy bumping into you."

"Oh, hello!" smiled Mrs Higgins. "The hospital got the pan off a treat!" She patted Max on the head. "But they said I should buy a *bigger* pan, so here we are!"

With that, little Sam peeped around Granny's cloak.

"Boo!" he giggled.

"Ahh!" beamed his mum. "You look happy!"

As Granny was telling her about their day, Pandora looked round for Max. She saw him sloping off towards the small, silver saucepans. *Uh oh…*

Pandora raced over. But before she could stop him, Max grabbed a saucepan and crammed it on his head.

"I AM A PAN HEAD FROM MARS!"

he said in a very loud alien voice.

Mrs Higgins spun round. “I don’t believe it!” she cried.

She dashed across to her son. But it was too late. The pan was already stuck!

“Oh, no! Oh, *Max*!” she said with a groan. “*Not again!*”

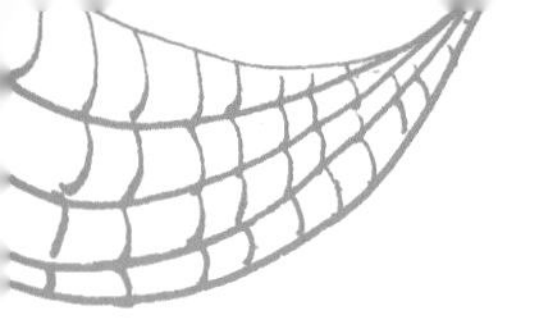

Slowly, Mrs Higgins turned to Granny. "Um, would you mind just looking after Sam a bit long—"

"No!" squeaked Granny. "I mean – I can get the pan off!" She stuffed her hand into her wand-pocket. But only to find it … empty.

Then they heard a loud cry.

"Gooo-baa!"

And they turned to see Sam toddling into the *underwear* department.

In his hand was Granny's wand, that was shooting out sparks as he waved it wildly about.

Suddenly pants were flying *everywhere*!

"SAM!"

WELCOME to CAMP CHAOS!

Chapter One

Bluebell glared at the hairy brown lumps lying in the grass.

"Ewww!" she shuddered. "I'm not touching that. It's *poo*!"

Pandora and her friends were at Wild Wilderness Camp in a big, dark wood. They'd been there all week doing lots of tasks to win them their Explorers Badges. Wildebeest Jones, their bossy camp

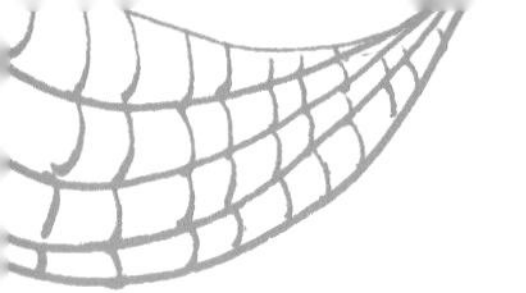

leader, was really, really strict. She'd *only* give them their badges if *all* their tasks were done very well. And this morning their job was to find out what owls *ate*…

"But Bluebell," said Pandora. "It's *not* poo, I promise. It's just *pellets* that the owls cough out. How will we know what they had for supper if we don't search through their pellets?"

"Maybe just *ask* them?" Granny shrugged. "Here – watch!"

She whistled loudly and a big fluffy owl swooped in and perched on her arm.

"Now then, dear," Granny said, "might you tell us what you had for supper?"

Blinking, the owl started to hoot. And as he did, Granny waved her wand and his hoots turned into proper words!

"I had five fat worms and thirty beetles!" he boasted. "But I'd *love* to try mouse-on-toast. I got the recipe off Bob – but sadly we don't have a *toaster* … oh well!"

The children could hardly believe their ears – a real talking owl! They grabbed their worksheets and as he nattered on, they wrote down everything he said.

With that, they heard a THUMP! THUMP! THUMP! and the owl hurried back to its nest.

"It's *her*," gulped Pandora. Then up marched their leader.

"At the ready!" barked Wildebeest Jones.

Hairy-chinned Wildebeest looked like a yak. And she smelt of warm, damp trainers.

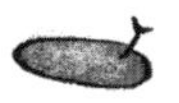

"Have you poked around in those pellets?" she snapped.

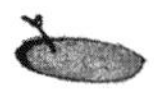

"Um…" gulped the children, and nervously passed her their worksheets.

Wildebeest checked them.

"Hmmm – good!" she said.

"And did you know," Pandora blurted out, "that owls would really love to have toasters?"

"What?" boomed Wildebeest. "Owls can't use toasters!"

"Oh, don't be too sure, dear," beamed Granny.

"What a hoot!"

Chapter Two

For their next task they had to be Nature Detectives, and find lots of plants and animals. Wildebeest had given them a very long list of things to spot.

Granny magicked up some gadgets to help them – magnifying glasses, compasses and really cool walkie-talkies.

"Off you go then, dears!" she said. "And have fun!"

The children raced away through the tall grass to see what they could find. But playing with their *gadgets* was actually much more fun!

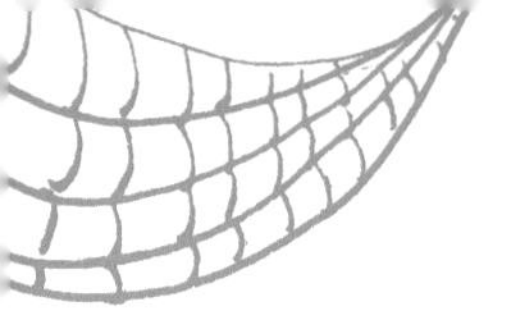

"Pandora to Nellie!" Pandora giggled into her walkie-talkie. "Have you spotted anything good yet?"

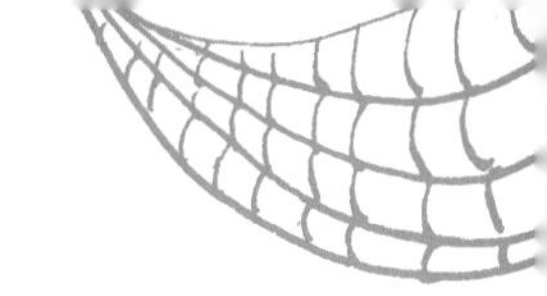

"Nellie to Pandora!" Nellie cried. "Yes, I have. I've found a Pan-dora-saurus!"

"A what?" gasped Pandora.

Nellie tapped her shoulder. "You!"

They carried on searching – uphill and down, round trees, under rocks, and in caves.

But although they found lots of plants, where were all the *animals*…?

Finally, the children sat down on the bank. "We'll never get our badges if we don't find some animals," Pandora said to Granny.

"Hmmm," said Granny. "Sometimes woodland creatures are shy. They're there, you know, but *hiding*. Lucky I know *just* the thing to get them out!"

Granny got to her feet and hurried around, gathering up things off the ground. Then she gave out all the bits she'd found to the children.

Pandora had grass, Jake and Bluebell had rocks and a couple of nice straight sticks, Clover had a seed-pod, and Nellie had two shiny pebbles.

"Now then," said Granny, "you must use your things to make some lovely music. I'll help too, and just you see what happens!"

She counted to three and the children began. Pandora got different notes from her grass by blowing it between her fingers. Jake and Bluebell tapped their drum-rocks, Clover shook her seed-pod which rattled, and Nellie clanged her pebbles like two shiny cymbals – TING TING!

As they played, Granny conducted. She waved her wand and stars danced out and swirled round all the trees.

Then all kinds of animals scurried out of their hidey-holes to listen to the magical symphony!

When the music ended, the children spotted every single animal on their list!

Even better, the animals weren't shy any more, and even let the children *play* with them.

“I LOVE squirrels!” Pandora cried. No one played off-ground-tag quite like them!

“Whoopee!”

Next the children had to build a raft and paddle it across a lake to an island.

Nearby, some other groups were building rafts too. Granny soon spotted her two witchy friends, Gwendolyn and Tilda. Gwendolyn was there with her grandson, Merlin. And Tilda was helping her granddaughter, Opal, and her group.

"Coo-ee!" called Gwendolyn, waving to

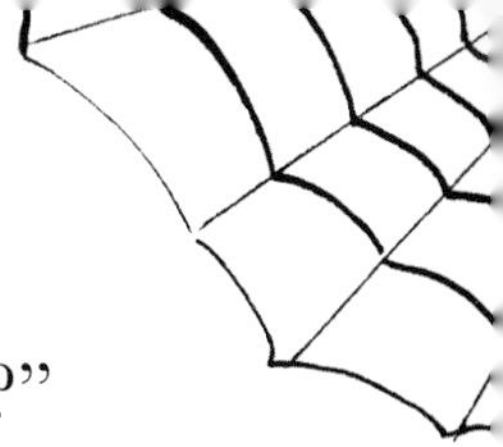

Granny. "Fancy a *race* to the island?"

"I do!" tittered Tilda excitedly.

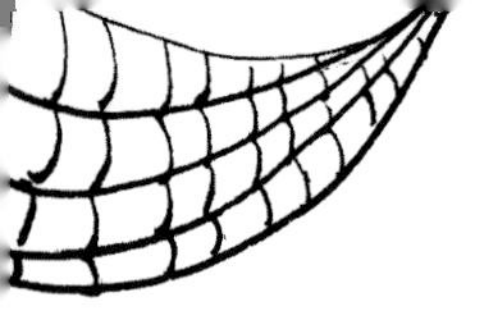

"OK!" Granny nodded. "You're on!"

Quickly, she helped her group gather logs and whispered tips as they tied them together.

"Nice and tight," said Granny. "And double-knot the ties!"

Pandora's group's raft was finished first and they placed it on the lake and got on. Jake and Pandora then used branches as oars and started to row them across.

"Bye-eee!" called Granny, waving back to her friends with a smile.

Everything was going really well. But then – halfway over – BLOOP, BLOOP, BLOOP – big bubbles began popping up all around the raft.

"Do you think it's a really big fish?" gasped Jake.

"Or what if we're *sinking*!" squeaked Pandora.

"Sinking!" gulped Granny. She reached for her wand. But pulled out some *seaweed* instead.

"There's water in my pocket!" Granny cried. And down went their raft – GLUG, GLUG – SPLASH!

They swam back to shore and squelched up the bank. They were cold, and wet, and smelled of fish.

"And what about our *raft*?" Pandora groaned. Now they'd have to start it all over again!

With that, Granny glanced across to her friends. But suddenly her jaw dropped.

Tilda's group were now crossing the lake on a *rope-bridge*. Except the bridge had NOT been there before!

"And look!" cried Jake. Gwendolyn's group had suddenly found themselves a rowing boat!

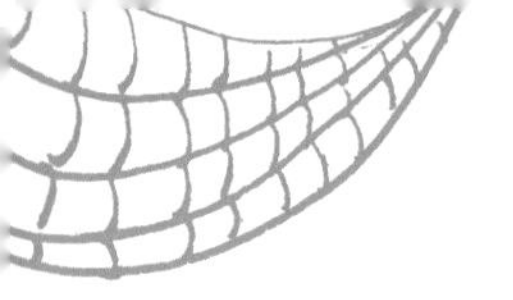

"How come?" said Pandora.

"Magic!" cried Granny.

At once Granny whipped *her* wand out too. If *they* could use magic, so could she!

BANG!

And suddenly a *speedboat* appeared with a giant engine on the back!

"In you all get, then!" Granny smiled. "Chop-chop!"

Everyone jumped in, put on their helmets, and Granny started the engine.

"Woo hoo!" she cried as the speedboat zoomed off, making supersonic ripples and waves. If Gwendolyn and Tilda wanted a race – they'd *get* one!

"Hooray!" cheered the children, reaching the island in record-breaking time.

Now they *just* had to find an interesting object to show Wildebeest when she came. And if she liked it – they would get their badges at last!

"How about this, dears?" Granny said, picking up a big broken eggshell. "This is a *dinosaur* eggshell, you know!"

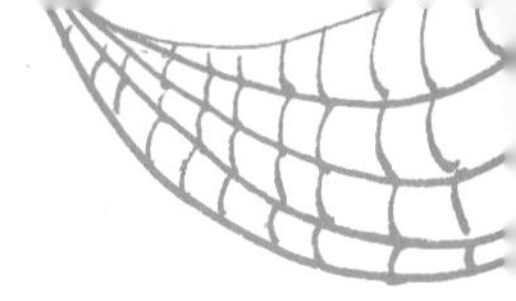

"It isn't!" laughed the children.

"Is too!"

"So where is the *dinosaur* then?" grinned Pandora. Granny was teasing – she knew it!

"Ah, well—" Granny started.

But suddenly she stopped as the ground started shaking, and a giant THUMP! THUMP! filled the air.

"The d-dinosaur!" squeaked Clover. "It's coming to get us – quick – hide!"

They dashed away to find good hiding places. Pandora and Nellie raced into a cave, Jake and Clover scrambled up a tree, and Bluebell and Granny camouflaged themselves in a bush!

They waited as the thumping got louder and louder.

Then up stomped the dinosaur – a really ugly one.

"Look!" cried Pandora, and she burst into giggles…

It was Wildebeest!

Everyone came out of their hidey-holes and Pandora handed Wildebeest the eggshell.

"Our interesting object," the children said.

But would it be interesting enough for Wildebeest? Or would they fail the task and not get their badges? Uh oh…

"Hmmm," grunted Wildebeest, looking at the eggshell. "A duck egg – but rather nice markings."

She thought for a moment, scratching her hairy chin. Pandora crossed her fingers tightly.

"So…?" squeaked the children.

"So…!" repeated Wildebeest.

Then slowly, she held out her hand – in which sat five shiny badges!

"Wow!" cried the children. They could hardly believe it. They were real Wilderness Explorers!

"Bravo!" cheered Granny, clapping her hands. "Well done!"

When Wildebeest left, Granny had an idea.

"Let's celebrate with cake!" she smiled.

She whipped out her wand. But before she could wave it, Gwendolyn and Tilda appeared. Merlin and Opal had got their badges too and they all looked really happy.

"Sorry about earlier," Gwendolyn said.

"Me too…" nodded Tilda, blushing.

"No hard feelings!" Granny smiled.

"So, how about that cake, then?" Pandora chipped in.

"I'll do it!" cried all three grannies at once, and – *POP! POP! POP!* – big, flashy cakes appeared all round the wood. When it came to *magic*, they were show-offs – but Pandora didn't mind.

Because, when it came to *cake*, the more to explore the better!